E   80-125

Sundgaard, Arnold

Jethro's Difficult Dinosaur

JETHRO'S
difficult
DINOSAUR

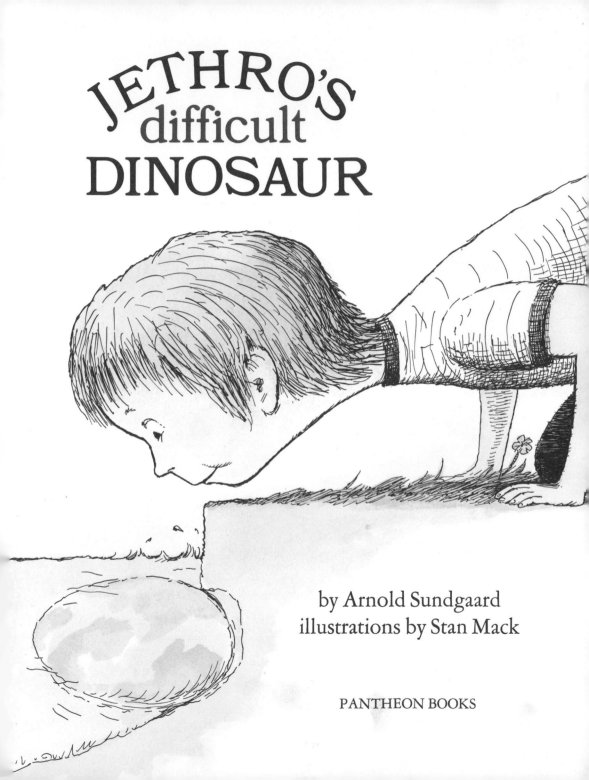

by Arnold Sundgaard
illustrations by Stan Mack

PANTHEON BOOKS

To Melanie and Maren

Text Copyright © 1977 by Arnold Sundgaard. Illustrations Copyright © 1977 by Stan Mack. All rights reserved under International and Pan-American Copyright Conventions. Published in the United States by Pantheon Books, a division of Random House, Inc., and simultaneously in Canada by Random House of Canada Limited, Toronto.

Library of Congress Cataloging in Publication Data Sundgaard, Arnold. Jethro's difficult dinosaur. Summary: Once the egg Jethro found in Central Park hatches, it proves to be an unusual but difficult pet. [1. Dinosaurs—Fiction. 2. Stories in rhyme] I. Mack, Stanley. II. Title. PZ8.3.S963Yo 811'.5'2 [E] 76-29616 ISBN 0-394-83301-5 ISBN 0-394-93301-X lib. bdg. Manufactured in the United States of America. 0 9 8 7 6 5 4 3 2

IN Central Park one summer's day
Young Jethro heard a lady say,
"That egg's the strangest egg I've seen—
It's salmon pink and bottle green!"

That's all she said, she said no more,
While walking past the northern shore,
The northern shore of Belvedere,
The lake that he was playing near.

Floating at the water's edge,
Just below a rocky ledge,
Young Jethro saw the egg as well.
What kind of egg he could not tell.

An ostrich, goose, a swan, a hen?
He wondered how and why and when
An egg like that had gotten there.
It might have fallen from the air!

Its mother's gone—where can she be?
I think I'll take it home with me.

He leaned far out and scooped it up—
Its shell was smooth as a coffee cup.

He placed it in his baseball mitt,
And there he deftly balanced it
While racing home to Gracie Square.

And in his room—his secret lair—
He had a shelf for souvenirs,
Things he hoped to keep for years,
Things he guarded with his life—
A scallop shell, an ivory knife,
A turbaned prince, a painted pig,
A wind-up clown who danced a jig.

That night his sleep was broken by
A dream of geese all flying high.
Each dropped an egg upon his bed
That hatched a gosling on his head.

While from the shelf the lady spoke
(He dreamed he'd see her when he woke)
"This egg's the strangest egg I've seen—
It's salmon pink and bottle green!"

Six weeks went by, and one day more,
When Jethro, coming through the door,
Saw the egg was gone. No, not quite,
But what he saw gave him a fright.

The egg was shattered, the clown upset,
And half the table dripping wet,
While perched upon the window nook
A creature with a puzzled look.
It seemed to smile, he could not tell,
And then his mother heard him yell.

She came up running to the door,
She knew at once—A DINOSAUR!

And then she cried in sheer dismay,
"I wonder what your father'll say."

His father sternly spoke, "Oh, no,
That dinosaur will have to go!"

"They need protection," Jethro said,
"I understand they're mostly dead,
And if this house can't be a friend
To beasts like that then that's the end.
I'm sure they wouldn't make a fuss
If we were them and they were us!"

So Jethro kept the dinosaur.
Each day it grew a foot or more.

And at the end of seven days
Was seven feet of beast to raise.
And seven feet of beast to feed,
Which is a lot of beast, indeed.

He built a stall beside his bed,
And fed the beast on crusts of bread.
With noodle soup and bales of kale
To keep the beast from looking frail.

Within a month one toe alone
Was bigger than an ice-cream cone.
One foot could fill a garbage can,
His tongue was like a frying pan.

And when he walked he'd clink and clank
Just like an ancient army tank.

He was a friendly sort of beast,
But my, the way his size increased!
Until they had to break the walls
And let him occupy the halls.

And all the other bedrooms, too,
Which was an awkward thing to do.

Because the family had to sleep
Upon the roof which was so steep
that they kept falling off.

One night the creature snored so hard
He blew them clear across the yard.
And left them clinging to the trees,
While wondering whence the sudden breeze.

And when this happened Jethro knew
He'd have to give it to the zoo.

And there it lived—to be succinct—
Until the beast became extinct.

But you can see it every day
On Central Park across the way.

GIFT OF
YOUNG
JETHRO